To Pa,

Catch Your Falling Star

With Love.
Best wishes
Christiane.
xo.

Catch Your Falling Star

Christiane Banks

CATCH YOUR FALLING STAR

Copyright © 2023 Christiane Banks.

All rights reserved. No part of this book may be used or reproduced by any means, graphic, electronic, or mechanical, including photocopying, recording, taping or by any information storage retrieval system without the written permission of the author except in the case of brief quotations embodied in critical articles and reviews.

This is a work of fiction. All of the characters, names, incidents, organizations, and dialogue in this novel are either the products of the author's imagination or are used fictitiously.

iUniverse books may be ordered through booksellers or by contacting:

iUniverse
1663 Liberty Drive
Bloomington, IN 47403
www.iuniverse.com
844-349-9409

Because of the dynamic nature of the internet, any web addresses or links contained in this book may have changed since publication and may no longer be valid. The views expressed in this work are solely those of the author and do not necessarily reflect the views of the publisher, and the publisher hereby disclaims any responsibility for them.

Any people depicted in stock imagery provided by Getty Images are models, and such images are being used for illustrative purposes only. Certain stock imagery © Getty Images.

ISBN: 978-1-6632-5670-6 (sc)
ISBN: 978-1-6632-5674-4 (e)

Library of Congress Control Number: 2023918583

Print information available on the last page.

iUniverse rev. date: 10/27/2023

For my six beautiful grandchildren,
Archer, Dollie, Hudson,
Huxley, Kristen, and Michaela.
With love.

Contents

Preface ix
Acknowledgments xiii

A Letter to an Irish Gentleman 1
Jimmy Fairy Dust 7
Thank You for Being My Friend 9
The Special Years 13
Mother's Day Story for Everyone 16
The Cross 20
A Walk to Wark 24
La Grande Soup 28
Beautiful Boy 33
Priceless Gift 36
Blessed Bradley 39
Weeping Window 46
Harvest Moon Groom 50
Hello, Dolly! 54
Will Be Yours and Yours and Yours 58
We Will Remember Them 61
Godspeed, Your Majesty 65
Needlepoint 68

The Other Christmas Miracle 72
Anam Cara 78
The Christmas Cake 82
Waiting for God 86
I Left My Soul in Fields of Silk 89

Bibliography 95
About the Author 97

Preface

Catch a falling star and put it in your pocket. Save it for a rainy day.

—Paul Vance and Lee Pockriss

In December 1957, Perry Como released the famous song "Catch a Falling Star."

Whenever I hear the tune, I travel back to 1958, when I was four years old, to my family home in

England, where I lived with my mom and dad and seven brothers and sisters on a street of terraced houses. I see high ceilings in our living room, the enormous windows allowing the light to flood the room, showing original ornate crown molding and a black-and-gold-marble fireplace with a warm glowing fire burning. Indeed, it was the best room in the home. But unfortunately, my siblings and I were not allowed to enter the room without a adult. Under the lid were a record and radio. I was mesmerized by the music maker hidden in a cupboard and the song "Catch a Falling Star." My dad had been fascinated, too, and purchased the EP.

We would slip away and play the record on the gramophone, then look toward the sky for the falling stars. Dad would catch them and at the end of the song open a pocket full of twinkling stars for me to see and choose one. A perfect memory gave me the title of this book.

I am a storyteller. My passion is to share stories that find me—the ones I keep close to my heart—and when appropriate, I will share them. This book is a collection of heartfelt short stories, most of which are true and many of which I have either been told or experienced firsthand. I have met some of the most remarkable individuals throughout my life. I have listened to many voices. These cherished stories need to be saved and shared. Each of the stories here is meaningful, with an individual message of hope, redemption, magic, blessing, and, yes, even a little fairy dust. It's a universal gift of love. So hold your hand out and catch your falling star.

Thank you for reading. I hope these stories bring you comfort and joy.

Acknowledgments

Thank you, Victoria Mininni, for the book cover design and for your other extraordinary gifts.

Many thanks to my three angels, Kathryn Riddell, Kathy Peruscello, and Kym Martin, for your faith and ongoing support, and to you, my readers, family, and friends. I am indeed blessed.

Keep looking up and catch your falling star.

A Letter to an Irish Gentleman

Always stay humble and kind.
—Lori McKenna

During the early 1960s, my mother was very ill. There were eight children to care for, all under fourteen—a mammoth task that no one person could manage. Therefore, an orphanage convent took care of us. Although we weren't orphans, we experienced life as orphans for several months. We eventually returned home to our mother after she recovered. The following text indeed captures a significant and memorable event in my life, and I am pleased to share it with you, as it conveys that it's always a good time to tell someone how you feel. Sadly, Irish singer-songwriter Val Doonican passed away shortly after I sent him this letter. I was certainly blessed with regard to my timing, as this delightful correspondence remains for all to read. The first letter is what I sent to the late Mr. Doonican. The second is his response to me.

Dear Mr. Doonican,

> This letter is being written to you by a mature adult but through the eyes of a young child as she saw you forty-five years ago. I was that child.
>
> Forty-five years ago, my siblings and I lived in a convent in Newcastle upon Tyne in England. Life in the home was a daily routine of tasks and assignments the sisters gave. No one paid much attention to us as individuals, as there were not enough

sisters and never enough time. We were directed to get on the bus outside one day after school. This we did with great anticipation and excitement. We asked Sister where we were going. She said that a very kind man called Mr. Doonican was singing at Newcastle City Hall tonight and he arranged for the children to attend.

As you know, the children sat around Mr. Doonican so that we were facing the audience. Approximately three thousand eyes were on Mr. Doonican himself. To everyone's enjoyment, Mr. Doonican began his outstanding performance. Later in the show, he stopped singing, explaining to his audience that they would have to excuse him.

"I have something most important to do." Then, climbing off his stool, he picked up his guitar and turned his seat to face us, the children.

He said, "Good evening, children. How are you? Now it is your turn!"

Mr. Doonican sang three songs, "Delaney's Donkey," "Paddy McGinty's Goat," and "The Marvelous Toy." We were asked to participate, and we did with great vigor and enthusiasm.

Never in my young life had anyone made me feel so special. It was a glorious moment for me. I had the best seat. I was facing you, and although I was young, I could sense your kindness and sincerity toward the children through your songs and your smile.

Today I would like to share with you that that moment has stayed with me all the days of my life, even to this day. I have told the story many times, and each time I have told the story, I think about how grateful I was (and still am) for your kind, sweet, gentle, extraordinary gifts.

My children and grandchildren now sing those songs, and I want to express my heartfelt thanks for an extraordinary moment that lives on and on.

Christiane

Dear Christiane,

How nice to read of your forty-five-year-old memory of Newcastle City Hall. Despite the passing years, I still recall the occasion very well. Mind you, I had no idea you were one of my backing vocalists. Thank you!

A young priest from St. Mary's Church in Sunderland was a good friend to us theater folk around that time, and he came to ask me for help. The nearby village church in one of the small villages had been damaged by a fire badly and needed some funds to repair the roof, hence the concert!

The same priest still remains a dear friend and recently enjoyed his eighty-fifth birthday. Incidentally, he celebrated our daughter's weddings and indeed christened our grandchildren. Some years ago.

I am sending him a copy of your letter. I am sure it will be as welcome in his home as it has been in the Doonicans' house.

I have spent over sixty wonderful years in the music world, and I still get a great kick from letters such as yours.

Thank you again, Christiane. Much love to you and your family.

Sincerely,
Val Doonican

Jimmy Fairy Dust

We all need a little fairy dust in our lives!
—Christiane Banks

"Jimmy Fairy Dust" is a story I heard growing up as a child. It is a fable, not a true story. I was born and raised in the mining town of Newcastle upon Tyne when most of the population worked down the mines, and it was a rough life for all the men and boys who spent their days and nights digging coal. I love this story of Jimmy and his abiding faith in such challenging circumstances.

Jimmy was a hardworking family man who lived in the northeast of England. He worked daily in the mines—deep down in the earth's bowels, digging out coal—a grueling and challenging job.

Every day on his way to work, Jimmy passed his parish church, where he would momentarily stop and open the old creaking door enough to step inside, doff his cap, and say, "Hello, Jesus! This is

Jimmy." Summer, winter, spring, and fall, hail, rain, shine, snow, and frost, Jimmy walked to work six days a week. And every day, he would stop at his church, pop his head around the door, and quietly say, "Hello, Jesus! This is Jimmy."

One day, he became sick with pneumonia and could not work or walk to his church. Jimmy returned to his church when he recovered, stopping on his way to work to say, "Hello, Jesus! This is Jimmy. Sorry I was away. I missed you!"

Eventually, Jimmy retired. Still, part of his daily ritual was walking up to the church, stepping in, and saying, "Hello, Jesus! This is Jimmy."

Inevitably, the passage of time took its toll, and one night, Jimmy died peacefully in his sleep.

When Jimmy approached the gates of heaven, he heard a voice calling in the distance, "Hello, Jimmy! This is Jesus."

I love this story. Its simplicity gives it a wonderful sense of accomplishment and resolution. Although Jimmy, similar to most of us, is a simple person working hard to look after his family, he is loyal, tenacious, and hardworking, never giving up on his gift of faith.

It has a fairy-tale ending. I think that's what I like about it the most. We all need a little fairy dust in our lives!

Thank You for Being My Friend

But if the while I think on thee, dear friend /
All losses are restor'd, and sorrows end.

—Shakespeare

He was in pain and knew he could be dying, but even in his last talk, Britain's treasured broadcaster Sir Terry Wogan was still the wry and witty man we knew and loved.

Most of you will not have heard of Sir Michael Terence Wogan. Those of you who have will understand why he himself was a falling star. For those of you who don't, please read on.

As a storyteller, I am fascinated by words and singer-songwriters. The Irish have a gift for storytelling. This star is included to keep Sir Michael Terence Wogan's essence close.

Terry first caught my attention in 1968.

I listened to my little transistor radio under my blankets late at night. I was fourteen years old and was supposed to be asleep.

I heard him on BBC with his lyrical, singsong voice and his brilliant humor.

I did not understand it, yet something about him completely captured me. I was hooked!

I followed him through the 1970s on BBC Radio. The program was called *Afternoons with Wogan*.

Who remembers "Fight the Flab" with Terry? "Gag the goldfish, blindfold the budgie, turn the baby's face to the wall" was his opening line!

Millions of women across the United Kingdom panted and stretched to his humorous exercise instructions for ten minutes. The program came on before the kids came home from school, and believe me—it created a lot more laughter than exercise. Terry Wogan felt like family, his Irish lilt telling stories and silly jokes on the radio, on cold winter mornings as we ate our porridge before heading out to school. Millions of listeners felt the same—we grew up knowing him as a friend.

When I emigrated to Canada in 1980, I was often asked, "What do you miss the most about England?" Of course, my answer always was "Family and friends, the North Sea, and Terry Wogan!"

Sadly, on January 31, 2016, Terry passed away. The tears that fell from the English and Irish came in such a deluge. I could hear them in Canada. What a sad day! As for myself, I wept!

Thanksgiving memorial service was celebrated at Westminster Abbey in London, England, to give thanks for Terry's life.

Family, friends, fans, and numerous stars came to honor him and pay tribute. But, of course, they also came to bid him farewell! Well deserved! As I lay under blankets in bed listening to the podcast through my earphones, bittersweet was the fifty-year-old sound bite that had Terry's giggles echoing throughout the church.

As Joanna Lumley proclaimed in a poem she composed for this occasion, "Oh, lucky cherubim and seraphim, / With breakfast hymns forever linked by him!"

I leave you with my gentle words:

> How lucky can the heavens be, as they still, to listen and rejoice!
>
> In the morning, when they awake, to hear his Master's voice!
>
> So long, farewell, goodbye, Sir Terry.
>
> Sadly, this is the end.
>
> One more whisper toward the sky!
>
> Thank you for being my friend!

The Special Years

> Just stay awhile in the special years.
> Their magic will soon be gone.
> —Val Doonican

As an author promoting my novel *Amelia's Prayer* and its sequel, *Amazing Grace,* I am privileged to encounter the warmth and kindness of the people I meet. It can also be a lonely and challenging job touring with my stories, not too sure who will stop to listen as I do book signings. This is a true story about three children I met several years ago. All three were under age twelve, each a wonder to behold.

This is one of the pleasures of my job as an author.

My thoughts from meeting these children were so moving that I am bound to share them with you now. The three children I met reminded me of some of the children in *Amelia's Prayer.*

Two of them were sisters who listened to me as I promoted *Amelia's Prayer* to their parents at a bookstore. I gave each of the children a bookmark and quickly provided a synopsis to the parents about the story, telling them that I was signing and gift wrapping copies of *Amelia's Prayer* that day in the store. As most people do, the parents smiled, thanked me, and moved on.

Later, the whole family approached me at the table. The young girls were so excited!

"We want to buy your book, please. Will you sign it?"

"I would love to sign it. Is it for you?" I asked.

"No, it's for our grandma. We think that she would love this book!"

It was a pleasure to autograph, gift wrap, and present the book to the sweet girls. I hoped my grandchildren would think of me so lovingly one day. Bless them!

Coincidentally, I came across another child with his grandmother in the same bookstore on the same day. I gave him a bookmark as I explained and promoted *Amelia's Prayer*.

"What is your book about?" asked the grandmother.

I gave a short synopsis of the story, and the young man surprised me, saying, "I would love to buy your book. How much is it?"

I told him the price, and he said, "I will save my pennies from my pocket money. Then I will come back and buy it from you."

I asked him his name.

"My name is William."

I thanked him for his interest, and his sincerity deeply touched me.

Later, William came to my table holding a twenty-dollar bill high above his head. He had a smile on his face from one ear to the other.

"I've come back," he said. "I'm here to buy your book. Would you please sign it for me?"

William looked so happy! It struck me that I sometimes underestimate children and their ability to understand what might be beyond their tender years.

After I had autographed his copy, I asked William if I might shake his hand to thank him for his support. It meant so much to me!

"How about a hug instead?" he said.

I can still feel his tender arms around me. It felt like he was trying to reach my soul, and it was the best hug!

Thank you, William; I will not forget you!

Mother's Day Story for Everyone

Behind all your stories is always your mother's story, because hers is where yours begins.

—Mitch Albom

You are loved, always with us, even when we cannot see you! We love you for all you have accomplished, seen and unseen, then, now, and forevermore.

I was seventeen when my mother died. It was shocking and tragic for my siblings and me, but we slowly recovered and moved on with our lives in time.

I had the opportunity to change my place of work. I moved across the river to Gateshead, working as a junior stylist at a department store. Most of our clients walked in. My first client was approximately fifty years old, and of course, when you are seventeen, that seems rather old.

I was permanently waving her hair, a process that took several hours. The client was quiet, and I didn't insist on the conversation. Eventually, she spoke to me in a relatively soft tone.

"Have you ever felt you've been here before, like déjà vu?"

I was surprised at her question.

"Yes, sometimes," I said.

"Many years ago," she continued, "toward the end of World War II, I was to be married. I had long hair to my waist and decided to have it cut and styled for my wedding day. I wanted the new

European look. The Eugène permanent wave from Paris, France, was the latest trend in hair fashion. The hair salons were open for half a day. Hairstyling was quite a luxury. I went to the salon on the corner of my street the day before my wedding. You can imagine how excited I was. A beautiful girl about my age then cut and styled my hair. It was a memorable day. The young girl shared my excitement, and my fiancé came to the shop to walk me home. He was a keen photographer, and he had a Brownie camera. So he asked the young stylist if she would take her photo with me outside …"

So special.

"I am sure you think this is strange," I said, wiping my eyes. "I believe the beautiful young stylist was my mam."

The lady smiled at me. "I thought so."

"My mam was a hairdresser working part-time in Gateshead during World War II. Unfortunately, she passed away several months ago. So I must tell you—I am sad and happy to hear this story."

The next day, the quiet lady came back into the salon and brought me the photo to look at, and there in all her glory was my mam, thirty years earlier, looking back at me.

> God could not be everywhere, and
> therefore he made mothers.
> —Rudyard Kipling

The Cross

When you saw only one set of footprints,
it was then that I carried you.
—author unknown

The following story comes from a longtime client and friend of more than thirty years, Frances, who lived in Holland. She told me this story herself many years ago, not long before, at one hundred years of age, she passed away peacefully sitting in her chair after a morning of shopping and an afternoon of playing bingo. During her long life, Frances experienced many challenging events: two world wars, emigration, the loss of her only daughter in a drowning, the accidental death of her husband, a mine explosion, and a personal battle with cancer. No matter what adversity she faced, she appeared to have a unique way about her that guided her through the tragedies in her long life—gifts of faith, optimism, and kindness. Frances shared this story as a fable, and it's one I've told many times. I think about it from time to time and would like to share it with you today, as "The Cross" is a story well worth telling, and helping to keep wisdom such as this alive is a passion of mine.

A long time ago, during the time of the Black Death, the inhabitants of a tiny European village high in the mountains were unhappy. They had suffered many catastrophes, enduring several decades of drought, floods, and the plague. Deciding something must be done to change their misfortune, the villagers agreed to assemble and pray to God for his merciful help. They prayed night and day. Eventually, God, in his mercy, said to them, "At sunrise tomorrow, come one and all to the village square and assemble. I ask each of you to bring with you your cross."

The next morning, as the sun rose gently over the mountains, it cast its warmth on the tiny village. Slowly, the doors of the villagers' homes opened, and the people made their way to the village square, each carrying a cross. Eventually, they stood together and waited. Finally, God called out to them, "Place your cross in the center of the village square."

The whole village—men, women, children, young and old, the lame and the blind, the weak and the robust—did as commanded. Finally, once the last person placed his cross, the villagers stood before a mountain of crosses, all of them unique: glass, wood, gold, jeweled, iron, paper, stone, pewter, silver, embellished, filigreed, and Celtic.

"Now, my people," God said to them, "join hands and pray in earnest for what you each need. When you have finished your prayer, I ask each of you to choose any cross you desire from the mountain you have created."

One by one, the villagers approached and chose their crosses.

Once the last villager took his cross, God said, "Hold your chosen cross high above your head toward heaven, displaying your choice for all to see."

All the villagers had chosen their original crosses.

Reading this story, I always remember that nothing in life stays the same—good, bad, or neutral. My friend Frances realized that and helped me understand by telling me this ancient fable. I like the idea of running back and grabbing my cross. It's precisely what I would do. What would you do? Moral of the story: your cross in life will never be heavier than you can carry.

A Walk to Wark

Where there is great love,
there are always miracles.
—Willa Cather

The story that follows is true and miraculous. The village of Wark does indeed exist, situated near the town of Hexham in the northeast of England.

Observing my sons as they navigate the path of fatherhood is the most rewarding experience. They've had the good fortune of having the shining example of their father to follow. I receive endless pleasure and moments of absolute wonder watching them all together.

I wish to share this father-and-daughter story from my experience some years ago.

When I was a young girl, one day, my dad came to me and said we were going somewhere special! For me, it was enough that he and I were going alone. I am one of many children, so going out with Dad alone was most unusual. We spent the afternoon in a tiny village called Wark—pronounced *walk*—situated on the banks of the Tyne. But if you blinked, you'd miss it.

I recall the sun's warmth on my face as we lay on the lush green grass of the riverbank. We talked about the little things in life—the reflection of yellow buttercups when I held them under his chin.

"How do birds stay in the sky? Where does the water come from in the river?"

My dad attempted to answer all my silly questions with great enthusiasm.

Later, taking my hand, my father walked me through the little village of Wark. We shared an ice cream cone, enjoying those lazy, luscious licks. It was idyllic, and throughout my childhood, from time to time, my father would come to me with a big smile on his face and ask whether I'd like to go to Wark for a walk.

Fifty years later, long after my dad had passed, one of my brothers died suddenly. It was a challenging time for my siblings and me because of the circumstances surrounding his death. The day after his funeral, I felt isolated, lonely, and sad while waiting in the airport alone as I traveled back to Canada from England. I wept.

A woman who appeared to be in her early seventies approached me and asked whether she could leave her bags on the chair beside me as she wanted to go for a cup of coffee. I nodded. The lady returned and sat down with her coffee. She started to chat and told me about how excited she was. She was traveling to Newfoundland and Labrador for whale watching and had done this for eight years. It was as though it were a pilgrimage for her.

She gently spoke to me about the color of the water. She described the icebergs as ten-thousand-year-old frosty giants rising from the ocean. She told me of the diversity of the birds, how the frigid wind burned her face, and how the sun's warmth made her skin tingle. Finally, she described the calm stillness of the area, the coolness of the air, and the outstanding beauty and magnificence of the whales!

The dear sweet lady had taken me to another world, and I forgot my troubles and sorrow for one brief moment. I told her it was a beautiful, extraordinary, and descriptive story. I thanked her and asked her whether she had traveled far and where she lived.

"I'm from a tiny little village about fifteen miles from here. No one has heard of it," she said and smiled. "It's called Wark."

La Grande Soup

Life is a beautiful dream, but don't wake up.
—French proverb

This is a true story about discovering my paternal grandmother—a gift to myself for my sixtieth birthday, possibly one of the greatest I have ever received.

Who we are is defined by those who came before us, our ancestors.

I was never fortunate enough to know my grandparents—a significant disadvantage as a child! Loving grandparents give young children a tremendous asset, helping them blossom and grow confidently. It is said, "One cannot miss what one never knew," but I can testify that it is untrue. Over the years, I have yearned to learn more about who they were, their thoughts and desires, and how they lived. Was I like them in any way? I longed to understand their tastes, talents, passions, daydreams, and more. You can discover as much as possible.

My mother was from Irish parents. They emigrated after the potato famine to Britain.

My father was born in Alsace-Lorraine, France, as one of two sons. As I was growing up, very little information was available about his earlier life; however, whenever I was in company with someone who could share, I asked questions and gathered information.

Nineteen years ago, on my fiftieth birthday, my husband and I met with several family members in Dublin, Ireland. We spent a fantastic weekend celebrating our Irish heritage! Several of my family members toured southern Ireland for several days. We were not alone. After seeing the Ring of Kerry (where it generally rains), we had a beautiful sunny window of time! Just as we finished our tour, it started to rain.

"Look at the rainbow!" my brother and I said in unison.

He and I were seeing opposite ends of the rainbow. I love the idea that it was a hug from our grandparents.

Several years later, we arranged to meet another family in the mountains of Alsace-Lorraine—exquisite. We toured through the village where my father was born and raised, eventually discovering that the home he and his family had lived in was now derelict, although it had a large garden. The neighbors were outside, and we asked them whether they knew anything about the family. My brother speaks fluent French, and he could interpret as we stood together in the garden, the French and English.

As we continued to inquire about our grandparents and father, one of the French family members suggested they had a great-uncle who might remember more about our family history.

Someone found the uncle and brought him over, and to our astonishment, he remembered my grandmother Jenny as an accomplished chef. Miming the action of her stirring soup in a great old iron pot with a giant spoon, he told us the story of how she made "La Grande Soup" and people came from all over the village to taste her famous soups. As a result, our family has several chefs—all known for creating excellent soups.

I had the privilege and honor to watch the others looking at him describe my grandmother. Observing my nieces as they listened, with tears, to the stories about their great-grandmother was mesmerizing. There is no question in my mind that my grandmother Jenny joined us that day in her neighbor's backyard. I could sense her with us and feel her pride, though she'd never held any of her twelve grandchildren. It was a sacred moment to cherish.

Later that evening, our family went to a restaurant in the village that resembled a Hans Christian Andersen fairy tale, where we shared traditional French food and drank the local wine from Roemer glasses with emerald-green stems. We ate onion pie, sauerkraut, and sausages and pear tarte for dessert. How I can still taste and smell the ambiance of the restaurant. We had a sensational evening—one never to be forgotten.

From time to time, I take myself consignment shopping. I derive great pleasure from meandering around the rooms, looking at all the beautiful merchandise, waiting for something to find me, and this day was no exception. Six beautiful vintage French wineglasses—Roemer, with emerald-green stems—were hiding in a cabinet in the back room. Now they are on display in the front of my china cabinet, and we use them regularly. They always remind me of the magic moments in France long ago.

Beautiful Boy

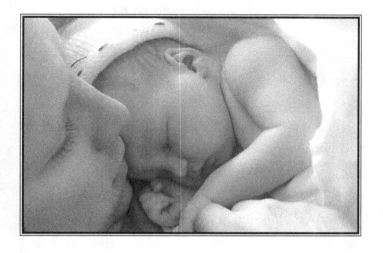

Close your eyes
Have no fear
The monster's gone
He's on the run, and your daddy's here
Beautiful, beautiful, beautiful
Beautiful boy

—John Lennon

So many gifts arrive with each grandchild, and I would like to share my feelings regarding that particular joy. This reflection about grandchildren also gives me the pleasure of sharing one of my favorite poems, "If—" by Rudyard Kipling.

I worked in the local hospital on the chronic care ward, running the hairdressing salon. But I often spent part of my lunch break looking through the glass window at the newborns in the baby ward.

The miracle of birth and the life of a new child have always fascinated me—the sublime perfection of the innocent baby.

Holding a babe in my arms for the first time, I am overwhelmed with gratitude. I saturate my senses with the feeling of love soaking up every detailed, glorious part of them—the perfection of the fingernails, as though manicured on their arrival. It's a moment that brings my being to center.

Seeing a grandchild, I remember pure joy and clarity holding their father in my arms for the first time years ago. Holding my babies has stood the test, unlike other memories, which fade as the years pass. Holding my grandchild is equally magnificent yet different and more emotional. I am older, and life and time have taught us how the ordinary is extraordinary. Embracing my grandchild personifies that.

Perhaps the greatest gift of all is the image of my child holding his child, instinctively loving him with a power far beyond his understanding. I rejoice at every moment I can observe my sons grow into wise and caring fathers as they nurture, protect, guide, teach, and love their children.

If you can talk with crowds and keep your virtue,
Or walk with Kings—nor lose the common touch,
If neither foes nor loving friends can hurt you,
If all men count with you, but none too much;
If you can fill the unforgiving minute
With sixty seconds' worth of distance run,
Yours is the Earth and everything that's in it,
And—which is more—you'll be a Man, my son!
—Rudyard Kipling

Priceless Gift

Flowers leave some of their fragrance
on the hand that bestowed them.

—Chinese proverb

The following is a true story about my son Michael. He was ten years old at the time, spending his pocket money on what I fondly refer to as a priceless Mother's Day gift.

During my career, I worked as a hairstylist in the chronic care ward of our local hospital. I was required to collect patients from their rooms and surgical wards and bring them to the salon, which was located on the second floor of the hospital.

One day, to my amazement, I came across a dear soul who, both arms in plaster, seemed stranded on the toilet and had been calling for help.

Looking straight into her eyes, I lifted her from the toilet seat and pulled up her pants as swiftly as possible. "I'm the hairdresser," I said. "I've come to take you for a hairdo!"

During our conversation that day, I learned the woman's name was Evelyn. I discovered Evelyn was a gifted artist, and we became great friends. She was like me, an English lady, an immigrant who lived in Canada. Evelyn was widowed, and she was an only child. She had no children. We spent many afternoons together talking about England. Evelyn was a very private lady and selective about her friends. She was not particularly enamored with children.

One late afternoon, as Evelyn was leaving my home after a visit, I watched my son Michael, then ten years old, follow her along the driveway. I observed that she stopped, they had a short animated conversation, and then they parted.

Several weeks later, on Mother's Day, Michael gave me a gift. I was thrilled to see the painting *Thatched Cottage in England* by Evelyn McDonald.

I love this story; I am honored to share this falling star.

Evelyn told me her perspective.

"Michael chased me along the driveway.

"'Mrs. McDonald,' he called. 'Could you paint a picture for my mom for Mother's Day?'

"I looked at him and asked, 'What would you like me to paint?'

"'Something you know she would like.'

"'I can do that. How much can you pay me?'

"'I can give you all of my pocket money for two weeks. That's five dollars.'

"'Done,' I told him. 'I will frame it for you, also.'"

Evelyn told me that in all her years of commissioned artwork, Michael Banks had given her the greatest amount of money for a painting relative to his income. Therefore, she was very impressed, and henceforth, the cottage would remain a particular favorite of hers and of mine. Thank you, Michael, and thank you, Evelyn.

The cottage hangs on the wall at the entrance of my home, a priceless star story hidden behind the frame—eventually to hang on Michael's wall.

Blessed Bradley

Blessed are the pure in heart,
for they will see God.
—Matthew 5:8

I have chosen this story because I love it. I hope you come to the same conclusion. As I have conveyed several times throughout this book of unique and precious stories, I have met many extraordinary people.

In this instance, twenty years ago, I connected to the lady who came to my door for a pedicure.

Marjorie was special to me immediately as she resembled my kindergarten teacher, Miss Boucher, from back home in England during the 1950s, who we all had great affection for.

Sharing this with her broke down her defenses. Instantly, I felt like her friend, as though we had a history. From time to time, connections such as this can happen, although I consider it a gift.

Marjorie looked keenly at her surroundings and brightly said, "You have a beautiful home."

"Thank you," I replied. "We love it. We have raised five boys here."

"It is a perfect place to run your business and raise a family, especially boys."

I agreed.

"Like you," she said, "I had a century home many years ago. My husband and I raised our children, three boys and a girl. My oldest boy, Bradley, is what we call a unique child now; however, in those days, sixty years ago, I had to hide him in the back room of my home. Anyone with disabled children felt ashamed." Marjorie wiped a tear from her cheek with the back of her hand as I handed her the tissue box.

"Thank you," she said. "Incredulous how the lack of education created so much heartache. Several other women in the same situation as myself formed a group. We worked tirelessly with the government and other industries and charities, corporate and private, to help us fund a support home for our special children, where we knew they would be safe, nurtured, and loved. Finally, we accomplished our home after many years of tries, tribulations, and tears."

As I massaged Marjorie's foot with lavender and lilac oils, she relaxed, stopped speaking, and turned her head to look out the window, letting her eyes rest on my favorite weeping willow tree, staring as if it might inspire her.

After a moment of stillness between us, Marjorie continued.

"Bradley and many young children like him who need specialized care have had a wonderful life, something I could not have provided for him had he stayed at our home. Although I spend as much time with him as physically possible, it is becoming more complex."

I was fascinated listening to Marjorie share her thoughts with me, trusting me enough with such a personal story.

"It must worry you now, particularly because you are both aging."

"That is very wise of you," she said. "Most people do not understand. My biggest concern is leaving him behind. It is strange to share with you, but I pray Bradley dies before me. He has come close several times with pneumonia."

"Does he know you?" I asked. "Does he recognize you are his mother?"

"Maybe." Marjorie smiled. "I keep sweets in my pockets. When I see Bradley, we play a game as he knows I have a treat for him. He doesn't show emotions, only when he is in pain. And when he plays the piano, it's a bit of a mystery to everyone. He plays by ear, smiling as he goes."

"I don't know him," I said, "so please forgive me if I speak out of turn. But Bradley knows what you mean to him and why you are there; you are his safe place, Mother's arms."

Marjorie smiled. "How do you have such insight?"

"I had a cousin, Peter, born severely mentally handicapped, a term used in the 1960s for Down syndrome. Physically, he was helpless. However, I knew he could feel it mentally, especially if I held him close and sang. I used to watch his dad hold him, and Peter could lift his tiny hand and touch his father's cheek.

"Again, Peter was a helpless soul on a physical level, but I believe he was the essence of pure innocence, even though he was seven at the time. Pure in heart and soul. Blessed."

"What a fantastic conversation," Marjorie said. "I don't speak to anyone like this. I am a very private person."

Marjorie moved toward me, reaching out for my hand and then pressing it to her heart.

"I understand the comment about Peter. Your story reminds me so much of Bradley. I must share a story with you."

Marjorie was excited. She sat up, placing her massaged feet on the floor. She looked into my eyes to share her story.

"Several years ago," she said, "the assistant caring for Bradley and his housemates took them on a boat ride along Lake Ontario. Bradley was in the boat and was staying close to the dock. It was a change, and Bradley felt the shift in the environment. Bradley was the last to be taken from the boat onto the pier.

"A stranger approached and spoke to Bradley. He nodded; it was as though the stranger recognized Bradley. The stranger held his hands over Bradley's head, blessing and kissing him on the forehead.

Someone took a photo at this very moment. Bradley has framed it in his room."

I was intrigued. "Who was the stranger?"

"Pope John Paul II. Now a saint!"

"I am so grateful you told me this story," I explained. As a Catholic, even as a human, I had tears in my eyes. "I have an affinity for John Paul II from when he walked out on the balcony to give us his first papal blessing. I can't tell you why I know he is an outstanding human being with the capacity to give of himself to the world, and I am not alone in this thought. Pope John Paul the Second is like our Queen Elizabeth II, genuine and dedicated to the people. If we all approached our lives and families with the same grace and decency, surely we might live in a more peaceful world. This story, Marjorie, deeply moves me. You were meant to come to me today. It's like a blessing from his holiness."

"As I have told you," Marjorie said, "I am a private person. I do not tell stories or talk about Bradley to anyone. I have astonished myself today; I feel so safe and comfortable here with you. It fell from my lips like a gentle prayer."

We both laughed and cried, sharing such a special moment, now a falling star.

When Marjorie left me that day, I realized what a blessing had occurred between us—and yes, blessed Bradley knows you, Marjorie, forever.

Bradley passed away peacefully in his sleep. Marjorie lived on for several more happy years.

Weeping Window

In Flanders fields the poppies blow.
—John McCrae

★ ✦ ★ ✦ ★ ✦ ★ ✦ ★ ✦ ✦

Eight hundred eighty-eight thousand two hundred forty-six English lives were lost, and many more were wounded, during World War I.

In the summer of 2014, I visited England. The world was preparing to recognize and acknowledge the one hundredth anniversary of the beginning of World War I.

Toward the end of our visit, my husband, Gary and I enjoyed spending Father's Day weekend with my younger brother Paul and his family.

We shared great food, wine, music, memories, and stories about our fathers. We discussed Dad's granddad's courage and their sacrifices before, during, and after the First and Second World Wars.

Eventually, our conversations and thoughts moved to the Weeping Window display at the Tower of London. This display consisted of 888,246 ceramic poppies, each one meticulously handmade. Every precious petal was made with respect, reflecting the memory of our fallen fathers, sons, brothers, uncles, cousins, loved ones, and all others who served—remembering the blood spilled on the battlefields and in the trenches, lost souls and the boys who never came home.

The Weeping Window display commemorated World War I's centennial, and each of the poppies was sold online. The proceeds were distributed among the various charities supporting the veterans and their families, and within hours, all poppies sold out.

This image of 888,246 poppies evokes overwhelming sorrow as I think on the individual lives lost, mostly males, and consider how blessed I am to live in a time of peace and harmony. Because of the sacrifice made, this image is one that can't help but reach out and touch each of us.

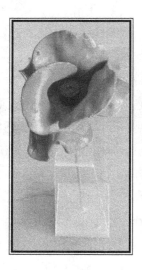

Toward the end of our Father's Day celebration, my brother presented me with one of the ceramic poppies from the Tower of London. I wept tears of every emotion. When others look at my poppy, they will experience that same feeling. Therefore, this gift will continue to reach and touch many for generations.

I pay homage to those who sacrificed all so that we may have the freedom to choose, the ability to laugh, cry, live, love, grow, and learn to live together in peace.

As the author of the poem "In Flanders Fields," John McCrae called Guelph Ontario home.

> In Flanders fields the poppies blow
> Between the crosses, row on row,
> That mark our place; and in the sky
> The larks, still bravely singing, fly
> Scarce heard amid the guns below.
> —John McCrae

Harvest Moon Groom

But there's a full moon rising.
Let's go dancing in the light.
—Neil Young

Several years ago, while visiting the state of Virginia, enjoying a glorious afternoon browsing the antique and bric-a-brac stores in the historic town of Williamsburg, I came across a small framed needlepoint craft whose quote struck me as poignant and gave me pause: "There's a special place in heaven for the mothers of boys."

I decided after thinking about it that it was much like the rhyme "A son is a son until he takes a wife; a daughter is a daughter for the rest of her life." Why?

I know there are many answers to the question; however, I would like to share this story—a wedding story. There is nothing extraordinary, though many mothers with sons will identify with it, and this is my gift to you.

I was driving my youngest son, Cameron, to some event many years ago. We were alone in the car, and I relished these drives with my boys; it provided time for us to talk one-on-one and for them to express their individuality. We listened to Neil Young on the tape as Cameron's passion in life was and still is Neil Young. Neil was singing "Harvest Moon."

"Mom," Cameron said, "when I get married, I will have this played for my first dance with my new wife."

"That's an excellent idea," I said. "I like that song; however, you may want to think about your new wife and her choice. She may not like Neil Young."

He smiled. "She wouldn't be my bride."

Twenty years after that conversation, Cameron found his lady love, and yes, she was a Neil Young fan! They lived together for a couple of years before they married and gave birth to a beautiful son.

When planning their wedding, Cameron told me with great joy, "Mom, 'Harvest Moon' will be our first-dance song, but not the Neil Young version."

Cameron has two brothers who are musicians, and they would serenade him and his new bride around the floor, singing the lyrics and playing the music on the guitar in harmony with Cameron's favorite song. He was thrilled; it felt like our unique story from when he was fourteen.

I had the idea to contact a friend, Suzanne, who is an excellent artist and also the mother of two boys. I commissioned a painting using my imagination and her imagination of Cameron and his lovely bride dancing under the harvest moon.

Suzanne and I spent many months discussing ideas and the journey of two mothers of sons creating a legacy and using art as their medium. Since I have only sons, I watch the groom and his mother first. It presents me with a unique story as all eyes are on the bride.

Experiencing my son's wedding day and watching him marry the girl of his dreams was the end of a chapter in our story as mother and son and the beginning of a new one. As his mother, I was the first woman he loved. I played an important role in how he respects, and nurtures his relationships with, his wife and all other women in his life. The father gives away his daughter, as does the groom's mother give away her son.

As I watch the grooms and their mothers at weddings, I am touched with a unique understanding of the moment. As the guests look toward the bride, I feel privileged each time as I witness tender moments between mother and son.

There's a special place in heaven for the mothers of boys.

Hello, Dolly!

This is a true story about a message from heaven!

September 7, 1965, was my first day of high school. Naturally, I was nervous while waiting in my new classroom with twenty other jumpy eleven-year-old girls. Eventually, our form mistress strutted into our classroom.

She had thick and shining dark hair and piercing black eyes. She was wearing a scarlet chiffon scarf that flowed behind her like Isadora Duncan's. She introduced herself with a soft Scottish accent.

"Good day, girls. My name is Miss Ferrier. I will be your form mistress this year."

She then stated to a class full of teenager girls in an all-girls school that the surest way to a man's heart was through his stomach!

Although I did not understand, I was utterly captivated. Miss Ferrier was like Miss Jean Brodie!

I loved her approach and persona when she spoke. It was like a song, and I was entranced. A feeling like this was my first experience of having an immediate connection to someone.

I was unsure how to negotiate my desire to be close to her, but then I had an idea. I approached Miss Ferrier and invited her to my home for tea, informing her that she should meet my mam. Although I remember her smiling, she said, "You may want to ask your mam first."

When I arrived home after school that day, I told my mam I had invited my teacher for tea. My mam did not receive this idea well at first.

"I don't want to invite your teacher for tea," she said. "I have enough to do!"

"But you will like her, mam, honest," I said.

I persisted over the weeks, and eventually, my mother gave in and agreed.

The great tea day arrived, and I was beyond excited. We arrived at my home, and I introduced Miss Ferrier to my mam. From that moment, they became lifelong friends, sharing many things. They had some beautiful times together, laughing, crying, and enjoying each other in friendship until the day my mam died.

I was fortunate to inherit custody of their friendship, staying in touch with Miss Pat Ferrier for many years. Sadly, my dear friend Pat eventually became ill and housebound. She lived in England. I had emigrated to Canada, and there was a time difference of five hours. So we spoke on the phone at 8:00 p.m. Canadian time, which was 2:00 a.m. in England, when Pat could not sleep from the pain she was in. We did this regularly, discussing many different issues, such as my mam, children, marriage, and husband, as well as *Amelia's Prayer*, which at that time was an untitled half-finished manuscript. Pat always insisted I finish my book because she was sure it would be special. She constantly told me how proud my mam would be of me and encouraged me never to give up.

We talked of life, death, and life after death, and those subjects we often don't discuss because of fear and the lack of insight and understanding. We discussed faith, courage, and whether there was a possibility to communicate after we passed on. Pat promised me faithfully that she would message me from heaven or wherever she may be to reassure me somehow all was well with her and my mam. Pat also assured me there would be no doubt in my mind that the message was from her and that I would understand it as such.

Pat passed away two days after that conversation several years ago.

From time to time, I would cast my eyes toward the heavens and ask Pat softly where my message was.

Finally, my son Michael and his partner, Helen, gave birth to a baby girl! She is simply miraculous, glorious, and perfect. Cradling her in my arms, I am overwhelmed by the overflowing love I feel for her when she looks through me as though we are old souls reunited.

Dolly Elizabeth was born twelve days late, coming into the world on November 2, 2016.

She shares her birth date with her great-grandma Doreen—my mam—as well as Pat, my dear friend and teacher. Both women celebrated their birthdays on the same day.

Thank you, Pat! Message received and understood.

Will Be Yours and Yours and Yours

> Love is composed of a single soul
> inhabiting two bodies.
> —Aristotle

In the third century AD, turmoil threatened the Roman Empire, and Emperor Claudius needed all the war power he could muster to save the mighty empire. As a result, he declared a ban on marriage. His theory was that single unmarried soldiers were more ruthless fighters than married ones. However, a Roman priest named Valentine believed marriage was a God-given sacrament. Therefore, he secretly performed marriage rights until he was eventually exposed and imprisoned for his crimes. Before his sentence passed, he fell in love with the daughter of his jailer. He asked for a pen and paper and then wrote a note to her. He signed it, "From your Valentine." Whether or not this is true, it is reported that the priest was eventually beheaded and named a martyr by the church. It is also said that Saint Valentine was executed on February 14, 270.

As the moments in my days flash by me, I have discovered, through time, that love is essential to me, especially when I consider love, loving, and lovers on Saint Valentine's Day and any other day.

It is not tangible, although it does have its place in society, creating a colossal economy during the commercial slump between Christmas and spring.

It is in what we do not see, touch, or even understand perfectly. That something, of course, is love in all its many facets! The look of love on grandchildren's faces when they run toward you with open arms. The reaction of my son's dog, Squire, when he hears his car in the drive—the dog's loyalty to him has taught me the meaning of loving a dog. So I believe true love never ends.

I enjoy people watching at airports arrivals; it's such a simple gift as we see all the varied versions of love.

Many years ago, I came across a poem so profound I inscribed it within me. Overflowing with selfless love, it personifies every version of that elusive word. Even though the story behind it is tragic, the words of love are divine and give a sense of hope and redemption.

"The Life That I Have" is a short poem by Leo

Marks used as a poem code in the Second World War. On March 24, 1944, Marks issued the poem to Violette Szabo, a French agent of the Special Operations Executive who was ultimately captured, tortured, and killed by the Nazis. The words to "The Life That I Have" were discovered scripted on the wall beside her bed after she died.

Its inclusion in the 1958 movie about Szabo, *Carve Her Name with Pride*, made it famous.

> The life that I have
> Is all that I have
> And the life that I have
> Is yours.
> The love that I have
> Of the life that I have
> Is yours and yours and yours.
> A sleep I shall have
> A rest I shall have
> Yet death will be but a pause.
> For the peace of my years
> In the long green grass
> Will be yours and yours and yours.

It was dedicated to all the loving souls who did not come home.

With love.

We Will Remember Them

Do not go gentle into that good night.
—Dylan Thomas

I wrote this for our hospital auxiliary's golden-anniversary book.

My first Saturday job was as a shampoo girl with a small hairdressing shop. Imagine the information women passed back and forth between hair dryers, washbasins, and teacups in those days! By massaging someone's head long enough, and with good intentions, I discovered that ladies often shared amazing stories and a wealth of information with me.

I immigrated to Canada and took a job running the salon on the chronic care floor of a long-term hospital care unit. During that time, I had the honor and pleasure of meeting many World War I and World War II veterans and war brides—most being long-term patients in the chronic care ward with various ailments like stroke, cancer, and dementia. One day, I cut an older gentleman's hair and chatted with him. I was aware that I often had a treasure trove in my chair! He told me he was ninety-eight years old. It was rare then to meet a man of ninety-eight who could converse with me about his memories.

"Have you seen active service?" I asked.

"Yes," he almost whispered. "I was at Vimy Ridge in France. Did you know there were ten thousand Canadian casualties, thirty-five hundred dead and seven thousand wounded due to the poison gas and wounds inside and out? Did you know that? Vimy Ridge was a defining moment in Canadian history."

"No," I said. "But I shall be eternally grateful for meeting you today and hearing your personal moving story. I am also honored to be spending time with you. God bless you always, and I thank you—grateful I have the opportunity to do so."

How futile and insignificant my words felt as I watched tears fall from his eyes onto his clasped and weak thin-skinned hands. My gratitude to him is my ability to tell his story, lest we forget.

One of my lady clients visited me one day for a permanent wave, which took a couple of hours! She was having a wonderful time, talking a mile a minute.

"Do you know I am celebrating my ninety-ninth year?"

She was excellent—the things she must have remembered, from the first motorcar to the first man on the moon.

"Can you remember your wedding day?" I asked.

She clasped her hands together, looking up toward the heavens. "Oh yes! I married in 1913. It was a beautiful, sunny day in June."

I asked what she wore, and her eyes sparkled as she answered.

"I wore the most beautiful dress in the world! I had seen it in a shop window in the city months before."

She explained that she used to stop in front of the window to look at it, saying aloud to no one in particular, "I want to wear that on the day I get married."

"I spent several weeks' wages on that dress—I shall never regret it," she said. "I walked down the aisle on my father's arm to join my future husband in that pale-blue chiffon gown that billowed like soft clouds. What a fabulous dress!"

She waltzed and danced around the little salon like a young bride dancing with her true love—a most tender and beautiful sight.

"He left for France the next year, in 1914, after he joined the army." She was quiet for a moment. "I never saw him again; he went missing in action. For so many years, I waited, hoping, praying—maybe he would walk through the door. Eventually, I accepted that he would never come back. I still remember that wedding day, floating toward my love in my blue wedding gown, him waiting for me with adoration in his eyes, shining an image forever pressed upon my heart."

Godspeed, Your Majesty

Godspeed, Your Majesty.

Queen Elizabeth II died on September 8, 2022, in Balmoral, Scotland, after reigning over us for seventy years and being the only monarch most of us have ever known. As individuals, her people from across the world are mourning her passing. I loved her, quite simply, and I want to share this story.

In November 2005, the Royal Command Performance was in Cardiff, Wales, at the Millennium Centre in the presence of Her Majesty Queen Elizabeth II and Prince Philip.

The Blue Man Group was among the myriad evening performances. Matthew Banks, one of our five sons and a member of the group, was honored to be one of the men performing for Her Majesty. So, naturally, my English family and friends were excited that night!

The following day, on the telephone from Wales, Matthew shared his experience with me in intricate detail. These are some of the highlights:

> We had rehearsed for over one week with lots of jocularities with all the performers, particularly the American ones.
>
> A regal hush fell upon the Millennium Centre like a gentle blanket on the performance day.
>
> When I first saw the Queen after our performance, she reminded me of my grandma in a tiara. Then she stood in front of me. I was overwhelmed by the majesty of her presence. I knew I was gazing upon a queen, one thousand years of regal royal history. It was one of the most amazing feelings of my life.

I will always be so grateful for Matthew recounting this genuinely remarkable story. Thank you, Matthew; we are so proud of you.

Forever our most gracious sovereign and queen, Her Royal Highness Queen Elizabeth II.

May kings and queens of heaven greet you and herald your arrival with trumpets, bells, and angels singing out welcome to Elizabeth the Great.

Rest in peace, Your Majesty, our one and only Elizabeth II. Godspeed, and thank you for everything.

Needlepoint

Out of clutter, find simplicity.
—Albert Einstein

The following is a true story. I had so much fun on this day and discovered the most glorious forgotten treasure.

One day, my lifelong friend Anna and I, along with our partners, arranged to drive along the Northumberland coast to Berwick-upon-Tweed.

We walked along the mysteriously rugged and stunning northeast coastline and saw the most beautiful and picturesque fishing villages.

We were resting to gaze at the dolphins leaping joyfully in the North Sea, Bamburgh Castle and the Holy Island of Lindisfarne in the distance—one of the most stunning, historical, and visually beautiful coastlines in all of England!

Later that day, we arrived at Berwick-upon-Tweed, in Northumberland. It is the northernmost town in England, located near the border of Scotland.

We had lunch in a theater restaurant overlooking the Tweed River, a unique and beautiful experience.

Later in the afternoon, Anna and I walked along the High Street, which had many charity shops, and of course, we popped in and out of each one.

The small cluttered shops exuded a stale, musty smell. They were stuffy, hot, and filled to the brim. Teacups, bangles, buttons, beads, boots, framed prints, silk flowers, big hats, old handbags, books, records—you name it, it was there. We dillydallied from one shop to the next looking for that one aha item. Alas, all to no avail.

Anna announced with a smile as she opened the door that this was the last shop.

As I cast my eyes around the musty, cluttered little shop, I could see a tacky old frame on the floor that held the most exquisite needlepoint work. It was the image of an old dresser, the type you would find in a farmhouse kitchen, and maintaining a white-and-blue willow-pattern dinner service.

Picking it up, I held it and wondered who would let go of something so precious, tenderly put together stitch by stitch with patience and love. I could feel it had unique energy!

There was no name, date, or story. Sadly, only abandoned history and beauty of this masterpiece of love, for reasons I could not fathom.

"Where will that go in your suitcase?" Anna asked.

I sadly put it down, and we left. We were walking to the coffee shop where we would meet our partners.

Anna stopped suddenly and looked at me. "Why not take it out of the frame?"

We ran back to the shop and purchased it.

Fast-forward from Scotland to Milton, Ontario. I had the needlepoint reframed in a manner worthy of this secret treasure. It is now proudly displayed on a wall in my home in Canada, over three thousand miles and one continent from where I discovered it, for all to see and admire.

A message to the creator of this masterpiece: Needlepoint radiates love and patience. Thank you. I love it, as does everyone who sees it.

The Other Christmas Miracle

Ring out the old, ring in the new,
Ring, happy bells, across the snow:
The year is going, let him go;
Ring out the false, ring in the true.

—Alfred, Lord Tennyson

December is an excellent time to reflect on the 2013 North American ice storm.

It plagued much of central and eastern Canada, parts of the Central Great Plains, and the northeastern United States from December 20 to 23, 2013, with large amounts of freezing rain and snow that damaged electrical power transmission capability, as well as much of the tree canopy. In Ontario, over six hundred thousand customers were without electrical power at the height of the storm. In the case of Toronto, over three hundred thousand Toronto Hydro customers lacked electrical energy or heat at the storm's zenith.

We were one of them, and this is my story.

I was in my kitchen listening to my favorite songs of the season, placing my grandma's shortbread recipe in the oven, and feeling that warm and cozy atmosphere. Yet looking out the window during preparations for the Christmas holidays, I could see the weather was dreadful, with ice storm warnings.

My husband and I were preparing for a farewell Christmas dinner in our hundred-year-old farmhouse—we had sold the home. We were anticipating a large family gathering, excited to spend time with loved ones.

Suddenly we lost all our power.

I was dashing to look outside to find out whether it was a street problem.

My husband and I were shocked as we looked around. Limbs and branches from our tree-lined driveway were strewn across the lawn, resembling a pile of toothpicks.

A giant tree limb was leaning on our garage door as though a tornado had hit us. A limb had snapped and pulled the main hydro line from the wall, and the wire left precariously dangling was live!

The same thing had happened across the road at a neighbor's home.

Sheets of lethal ice on the ground made us slip and slide. We were helpless. There was not much for us to do until the hydro company could come and help.

Realizing this would be longer than an hour, we went back into the house and made hot coffee on the gas stove—a blessing of all blessings throughout that week. The power was back on to the street late in the evening, except for the homes with disconnected wires. We were returning to our cold dark home using candlelight, curling up with hot water bottles and a ton of blankets on the bed to keep us warm.

The house was even colder by the morning of Christmas Eve. We were unable to leave. We needed to ensure the home was safe from frozen pipes and floods.

We were fortunate that the electrician who lived next door could help us fix the main line demolished by the fallen limb. However, an inspector needed to confirm it was safe before the power company could reconnect. Finally, the inspector arrived at four o'clock in the afternoon, looking exhausted. He told us he had worked day and night for days.

We asked him when we would have our power back. I smiled at him and suggested that if he could speed things up, I would slip him five dollars as I was expecting twenty-five guests for dinner the next day.

"Tempted as I am," he said, "you are entirely out of luck. Hydro won't be back to reconnect. So with only two of you, not this week, but next week, maybe. Thousands are without power. So many in the country are freezing, with no water or bathroom and no Christmas celebration."

"I'm sorry," I said.

I was feeling guilty and selfish. At least we had some form of heat.

"Merry Christmas," I said to him. "I wish you well. Thank you for coming and approving us."

The sun had slipped behind the trees, trailing that gorgeous late-December light. It gave way to the magic of Christmas Eve stars and the crisp air surrounding us.

"Merry Christmas to you," he said. "I'm sorry I couldn't be of more help." He smiled, waved, and left us as the last of the light disappeared.

We spent Christmas Eve, my favorite night of the year, by candlelight, keeping warm and deciding we would cancel everything in the morning.

Gary filled the four hot water bottles, and we headed to bed. It was the warmest place.

"I want to be alone for a while," I said. "I won't be too long."

I felt so sad wrapping up. I decided to meander the court; every house was bright with light. I could feel the warmth from within the homes.

Peeking inside, I watched the camaraderie and smiled. I was happy for them.

Nature, in her wonder, enhanced our old trees' crystal decorations hung in multitudes from the branches. Looking up toward the stars, I could see my breath.

A nativity display in a garden gave me pause, and I stopped and prayed.

Please keep those who are cold safe and warm, especially the little ones. If anyone is listening, please give me some power to host my last family Christmas in this home, if it isn't too selfish.

I was climbing into my warm bed, snuggling up to Gary, hearing the rhythm of his breathing and the yuletide songs playing from Westminster Abbey on my battery radio. I soon slipped into a peaceful slumber, having counted my many blessings.

Later, I was awakened from a deep sleep, startled. Sitting upright, disoriented, I found myself shielding my eyes from all the bright light as the loud noise from the clock radio flashed 3:00 a.m. December 25.

"Gary, wake up," I said, nudging him. "We have power. We have light, Gary!"

He jumped up. "Holy cow! Did you give the inspector five dollars?"

"No, I prayed beside a nativity display last night. Look—my prayers were heard. I was so sad to think we weren't going to see our family, and somehow my prayer was answered. And we will all be together."

December 25, 2013, will always be remembered as my Christmas Day miracle. We celebrated with family and friends, so grateful to be together. Everyone participated, producing a creative and delicious feast. Our home was frigid, but we all wore layers of clothes, happy to be in one another's company, all glowing from the inside out.

Anam Cara

> Let me cast my eyes upon you to calm
> the storm within this wandering soul.
> —Christiane Banks

Anam Cara is a book I read on Celtic wisdom by John O'Donohue. The title inspired me to examine the explanation for *Anam Cara* in the book, and I'm discovering the Gaelic meaning: soul friend. It reminded me of a true story I wrote many years ago, and I'd like to share it with you.

Throughout time, poets have endeavored to capture love's essence and the fundamental meaning of love. Whether poets or not, we all are no different—we all long to capture the many versions of the intangible meaning of love.

For several years, I worked on the chronic care floor in a hospital in a small town in Ontario. Many residents lived on the ward and required several hours of nursing care daily.

As we approach Valentine's Day, I'm reminded of Mary, one of these extraordinary individuals, and her husband.

One of our residents, Mary had been a schoolteacher, working in a one-room schoolhouse in the 1920s. She had been married for over sixty years to Claude, a retired gentleman farmer whose focus was now his wife. Claude would visit her twice daily, at lunchtime and at dinner, seven days a week. Mary would stand patiently and wait for her handsome hero at the ward's entrance.

During their sixty-year marriage, they overcame many obstacles. They traveled and loved life, and never having children, they enjoyed their nieces and nephews.

As they approached their September days, their increased physical separation would not stop them. Nothing could really keep them apart, and no Shakespeare sonnet or Tennyson poem has the ability to describe the love they exchanged. But the moment these two would part at the end of the day, I was able to observe the true meaning of love—a gift.

Claude was well over six feet tall. Although he was aging and stooping, one could see he had been a handsome man in his youth. Mary was quite the opposite—petite, and giggled like a young girl. She radiated beauty, especially when Claude was around; they were hand in hand. They would shuffle through the hospital's corridors like sweet young lovers, oblivious to anything outside their desire to give and share of themselves. I shall never forget when I first witnessed their farewell at the end of the day.

No moon, June, stars above, or hearts on fire for my true love. Simply this: Claude, standing tall, and Mary, petite, looking up toward her *Anam Cara*. Claude bent and tenderly kissed the top of Mary's head. Mary was too petite to reach her handsome prince and instead took both of his significant hands and held them, kissing each palm with a tenderness that left me breathless.

Should we all experience a moment of love like that, then we have touched the face of God.

I write this because I can still feel the power of that love and the glory of their commitment to each other. I witnessed the most profound truth that lies in the simplest of gifts. The moments they spent together inspired me to write a short sonnet:

> Let me cast my eyes upon you to calm
> the storm within this wandering soul.

Lay my shadows next to yours that we may blend in harmony with Earth's warm tones and together look toward the sunset lest it is only in my dreams.

You are my life, my breath, my soul until death, and I will find you in eternity.

I am sure they have.

The Christmas Cake

Be glad, be good, be brave.
—Eleanor Hodgman Porter

The following is a true story.

On a frigid Friday evening in late November 1969, a young girl worked alone in a tiny shop on a corner street. The apprentice hairdresser's boss left early, leaving the young girl to clean up and close the shop at the end of the day. However, she had yet to lock the door. The door opened, and a middle-aged lady appeared and pushed the door shut against the howling wind and the cold evening.

"Can you do a shampoo and set?" the lady asked with an Irish accent. "I understand it's last minute. I'm desperate."

The young apprentice was delighted to get the practice and help out. "Where are you from?" she asked.

"Northern Ireland, Belfast. I'm visiting a friend on holiday. So, yeah, I'm returning home tomorrow. We're going out tonight for dinner."

"My brother's there in Belfast," the apprentice said.

"That's a coincidence. Where does he live?"

"He's a soldier in the British army."

The lady was quiet as the apprentice carried on with her conversation.

"My mammy always worried about him. She sits crying whenever the BBC Radio tells us a British soldier is injured or even killed. I think she thinks it's my brother, poor Mammy."

"I'm sure she does," the lady sighed sympathetically.

"Is it scary for you to live in trouble?"

"Yes, it is, and like everyone else, I hope it stops soon and your brother can come home and make your mammy happy again."

They both fell silent, each holding on to her thoughts as the apprentice finished the job. Then, finally, the lady was delighted, paid the girl a very generous tip, and left the shop.

Several weeks later, on Christmas Eve, the apprentice's brother phoned the mother from Ireland to wish the family a merry Christmas. After speaking with his mam, he asked for his younger sister.

"Hello, kid," he said to her. "Last night I was on patrol. It was cold last night, miserable and dark, about seven o'clock, and my patrol was until ten, so I kept patrolling up and down, stomping my feet to stay warm. Several people were passing by with packages, boxes, shopping bags, Christmas trees—last-minute shoppers because it was the twenty-third of December. A lady approached me. Did she want some assistance? She was keen to talk to me about something!

"She asked me, 'Do you have a sister who is a hairdresser in England?' Well, you could have knocked me down with a feather.

"I said, 'Yes, I do.'

"She said, 'Fantastic—I believe your sister did my hair a few weeks ago. I recognized you. I was sure you belonged together; I was watching you. You know, something in your stature, stance, and voice. Your accent is like hers, but that's amazing.'

"I was speechless.

"'Your sister is sweet. She told me how worried everyone at home was, especially your mam, and how she fretted and missed you.'

"I couldn't help crying like a bairn as I thanked her.

"She said, 'I live close by, just a few streets away.'

"I was amazed that this woman recognized me in the dark fog the night before Christmas Eve, a touch of Christmas magic. She smiled at me and waved goodbye. 'Merry Christmas.'

"Imagine my surprise when she returned later that evening with a hot thermos of tea and a big hunk of homemade Christmas fruitcake, just like our Mammy.

"Smiling at me, she said, 'A little touch of home with love from your sister and mammy.'"

This world is a mystery and sometimes magical, leaving gifts exactly when needed.

Waiting for God

No one is useless in this world who
lightens the burden of another.

—Charles Dickens

"Waiting for God"—three simple words, but put them together, and they conjure up quite an image.

My career has taken me into many retirement homes as a beautician and foot-care specialist. In addition, I often work with clients in declining years. Elsewhere, these individuals tend to have no voice—often it's simply because they're old that we as a society no longer listen to them. So I am privileged to hear some of the most poignant, powerful, and enlightening stories. These outstanding individuals are waiting for God.

I would visit Rose once a month to provide a manicure and pedicure. Widowed, she lived in a retirement home, and in her ninety-five years on this earth, she had raised five children and had fifteen grandchildren and seven great-grandchildren.

On one of my visits, I asked Rose how she was doing that day; generally, she was cheerful and optimistic and would ask me about my children and family.

"I'm fine," she replied. "I'm fortunate I live in a beautiful retirement home. I have a lovely room with a pond view, good food, and excellent care. But, weary, I sit in my wheelchair daily, waiting for the good Lord to come for me and take me home. Every night I fall asleep praying for this to be my last day on earth. I ask only to be disappointed to wake up to another endless day of waiting. The good Lord, why do you keep me here? I have no purpose, and I cannot walk, I can barely see, I cannot hear ... I have had my time. Please let me go!"

I felt sorrowful as I listened to Rose.

"Finally," she continued, "yesterday, my door opened, and there stood my youngest son. As he slowly walked toward me, I smiled at him. I said, 'What a lovely surprise, my son. What are you doing here today?' He quietly continued walking toward me. Then he knelt at my feet and gently laid his beautiful head of black curls upon my lap, and we sat in silence as I stroked his brow with my gnarled fingers and twisted old hands—his mother's hands. Casting my eyes toward the heavens, smiling, I whispered, 'Thank you, Lord; now I understand.'"

I am constantly moved by the power and depth of a mother's love. So many stories and loving moments I have witnessed between mother and child. Fathers, also, only differently. Many of the examples I see rise above the meaning of love and show me the strength and the gift in faith. Waiting for God is one of them.

I Left My Soul in Fields of Silk

Take my hand, and I will lead you to a place …
in a land where peaceful waters flow.
      —Gilbert O'Sullivan

After thinking many times over how to conclude my book of falling stars, the story that follows is the crowning one, not necessarily because it's my favorite, or that it's the most exciting story. It's because it gives a voice to my thoughts as to why we are here—to love and to be loved, to discover, to always be kind, and to tap into a passion that drives us toward something outside ourselves during the little time we have here on earth. And honoring those who came before us, pioneering, fighting, and striving to give us the privileged lives we live today, let us follow their example for the little ones we will leave behind to navigate the future.

My maternal Irish grandmother has forever eluded me; I never knew her. We knew another family member had adopted her—something often practiced in Ireland during that time. Information was limited regarding the time before she married my grandfather and emigrated from Ireland to England. So we wondered whether her name, Catherine O'Shea, was legitimate. Occasionally, I would rummage through the old photos and any certificates I could find, searching for something that would bring us together.

On my fiftieth birthday, my husband and I met some family members in Dublin and traveled around southern Ireland. An older cousin had given me a copy of my grandparents' marriage certificate, which indicated the church where they had been married. My oldest brother, Michael, and I arrived in Limerick at the church of Saint Michael's on a cold, wet October night, only to find the church doors locked up with chains, padlocks, and bolts.

Standing in the fierce gales of Ireland and the relentless lashing rain, soaked to the skin, I had dreamed of standing inside the church in their footprints at the same altar where my grandparents, as a young couple, had exchanged their vows a hundred years before. Then, feeling desolate, we left the church, and I promised myself I'd return to it one day.

Many years later, in 2020, as my family celebrated Mother's Day and Father's Day in Canada, our children gave us the gift of a DNA ancestry kit. I was overjoyed. Karen, my daughter-in-law, explained to me that our son Mark came up with the idea of this gift, for which I will be eternally grateful. And so the magic begins!

Several weeks after I registered, including all my grandparents' names, I received a short message from a family member via the DNA company's website: "Who is the O'Shea?"

I had finally discovered Catherine O'Shea's family. Margaret and her daughter Paris live in

Florida. We have become close friends over the past four years and attempted to meet but have not yet succeeded. My newfound cousins in Florida gave me the name and telephone number of a cousin in Ireland. The lady's name is Joan, and she is the sister of Margaret from Florida. I contacted Joan, and we talked for several hours on the telephone. Joan invited me to visit with her the next time I came to England, informing me I would find many relatives in Labasheeda, as her father, my great-uncle, was one of seventeen!

In October 2022, my younger brother Paul and I made a whistle-stop visit to Joan's, arriving as the sun slipped away behind her quaint cottage on the banks of the River Shannon in the village of Labasheeda (meaning "fields of silk").

When Joan opened the door, I recognized her as part of myself. She looked like all of my mother's sisters—all three of them tiny—and looked up at me like a little doll as she said to me with her beautiful Irish lilt, "Well, now, come in—you're like one of me own."

We connected in an instant.

Joan showered me and Paul with warmth and gracious hospitality, showing me to my room, her best guest room next to her, and whispering, in that singsong lilt, that I had already come to love, that she had left the electric blanket on all day to be sure I was warm that night.

I need to share the power of those few simple words as I cannot think of any welcome that touched me so tenderly as Joan's desire to keep me warm. It seems such a simple thing, but the thoughtfulness of this act—keeping someone warm is such a fundamental expression of love—affected me deeply.

We all experienced this unexpected gift of joy, and camaraderie. In a short few days, we found what had taken a lifetime to discover. I found pieces of my soul in Labasheeda.

As I began this book with a star story, I end with this thought: Like a child, I look toward the star-filled sky now and then when I'm wishing for or dreaming about someone or something special. I wonder whether we all do from time to time.

Labasheeda has a starlike magic threaded between the lines. Its story and the absolute joy I felt in discovering my grandmother's family will live on within me and continue to glow like a shining star. My hope is that you will catch some of the same feelings as you read and reread these star stories and find yours.

I leave you with this Irish blessing:

May God be with us and bless us.

May we enjoy the laughter of our children's children.

May we know nothing but good luck, good health, and happiness from this day forward.

And until we meet again,

May God hold you in the palm of his hands.

Bibliography

A Treasury of Poems, compiled by Sarah Anne Stuart
Simple Abundance: A Daybook of Comfort and Joy,
    by Sarah Ban Breathnach
Romancing the Ordinary, by Sarah Ban Breathnach
Poem-a-Day: 365 Poems for Every Occasion, selected
    by the Academy of American Poets

Images
Pope John Paul II. Photo Credit: Rob Croes (ANEFO),
    Wikipedia Commons.

Songs
"Harvest Moon" by Neil Young
"Beautiful Boy" by John Lennon
"Catch a Falling Star" by Paul Vance and Lee Pockriss
"Where Peaceful Waters Flow" by Gilbert O'Sullivan
"The Special Years" by Val Doonican

About the Author

Christiane Banks elegantly assembles a diverse selection of intimate stories that provoke a myriad of emotions. From joy to melancholy, these personal anthologies will incite compassion and fill you with comfort.

In Christiane's words,

> I have had the privilege of meeting many intriguing people with extraordinary personal accounts to tell throughout my life. These stories

stand the test of time, and it is my passion to preserve and amplify these precious narratives. These timeless anecdotes are the falling stars that I have found and collected to share.

Catch your falling star and hang on to it.

Printed in the USA
CPSIA information can be obtained
at www.ICGtesting.com
LVHW091506111223
766123LV00003B/465